P ROLOGUE

Margo

The magnificent full and bright moon of the night coincided with the overwhelming cool breeze that was making the night a little too cozy and fun-seeking. It was as if the whistling of the wind was riding in competition with the subsequent rustling of the green leaves from the tropical trees. The exhilarated leaves, being a part of the nature that surrounded most of Tropical City, somehow filled the air that blew directly from the North with more than pure intensity. It made the night intoxicating and irresistible.

This made it almost impossible for people on the streets not to get quite excited with the sensitive night, or naked lovers in the silence of their rooms, moaning and groaning alike until the night is filled with their tireless lust. Married couples especially would never ask for anything better than a night like this; it was intoxicating, it drove them nuts, it had their hands tearing at each other's clothes and it made even the weakest of them too aroused to think of nothing but pure, sinful and energy-consuming love making.

At the moment, Margo Lattisaw could only think of her husband humping hard as he went mad with lust. He was going to share that lust with her while he insanely welcomed her home with a shove of his tongue into her mouth and a covertly drive of his old hardness into her warm thighs. She knew it was exactly what she needed immediately after spending the longest hours of her time at McAmzee Pharmaceuticals, a very old and still effectively functioning three-floors Pharmaceutical company that was now fifty percent hers to manage.

McAmzee had just made a very profitable break and soon enough, it would be handling major new drugs' marketing achievement or income hit. If things went accordingly, Margo thought, McAmzee would welcome a new dawn of shipping their new products to the entire world for sales. The new Ozone, designed to rid young children from extreme asthma, was already tested and it was that good – the whole world was going to be demanding for it nonstop. Well, Margo's thought wandered off again, another feeling that was nonstop at the moment was her need for a good fuck and an embrace from her husband, Grey, until the morning woke them up.

Margo smiled as she remembered that she had been married to her sixty-one-year-old husband for more than twenty-one years already. Grey had surprisingly grown from the unbearable douche bag that approached her in summer camp with a handful of mud that was meant for her white dress to a very compassionate and responsible husband and a successful retail manager at one of the City's biggest mall and outlet. It had been a crazy ride for her and Grey throughout their young days until one or both of them had gotten tired of the enmity, and then hitting the sheets settled the long years of scores to settle. A few years later, Grey had gone on one knee and she had cried out in ecstasy when he asked her to marry him.

"So much for saying yes." Margo thought aloud.

The twenty-one years with Grey had been the best part of her life. She knew that there really was nothing comparable with the overwhelming love that she still shared with Grey. For the best time of the long years with him, Grey had proven to be the only man that could make her feel fulfilled and contented. He gave her his unending attention, shared ideas and values with her, and never stopped whispering in her ears every night how much he loved her, and especially how much he wanted to have sex with her most of the night.

Margo felt the blood rush to her cheeks at the thought of the nights with Grey. He was the most compassionate man in her world and it was hardly unthinkable to have the imagination of another man in her head.

"So much for saying yes." Margo muttered again.

She had decided to walk home from the central park because of the way the night's breeze was making her feel. It clouded her thoughts and made her think of Grey and their bedroom alone. *Or was it just any man?* Margo shook her head and wondered why she was considering that she could think of any other man. She was quite sure a few seconds ago that Grey was the only man she could think of in decades.

"So much." Margo muttered this time around.

She was beginning to think about the warmness between her thighs despite the cool breeze and the cozy weather. She laughed when she remembered that how she was feeling was typical of women who were perhaps twenty years younger than she was. But Margo sincerely could not deny the fact that she was horny and the walking in the cold night was a big mistake. It wasn't shaking the feeling off, instead it was feeding the lust that was starting to consume the entirety of her thoughts.

Attempting to calm herself, Margo quickened her steps and glanced at the vaguely similar tall buildings that were at both sides of the street that she took. Each building was a modern twin story structure that apparently housed two or three flats on each floor for rent. From a particular window, Margo briefly sighted a younger woman who was pacing the room and was shouting instructions at someone. The woman suddenly stopped moving, batted her eyes incredulously at whomever was with her in the room, and then her hand went for the button of her shirt.

Margo quickly turned her head and attempted to look for something else to distract her.

"So much." She whispered again.

As she turned the last corner into the more urban street of the city, her eyes fell on the red bricks duplex that had been her home for far too long that she stopped herself from counting the days. The tended red flowers and green lawn that was the front yard of the house impressed her as she approached. They reminded her that there was a time when she spent most of her everyday hours thinking about growing the best delicate grasses and flowers in front of her home. Now that her front lawn was perfected, Margo couldn't believe that she was thinking of doing the same to the backyard.

"Home." Margo unashamedly whispered.

She was no longer thinking of the flowers or the long years that she had spent in the house. Her thought had wavered to the man that was waiting for her in their bedroom. She began to imagine immediately that he was having the same anxiety and couldn't wait to jump on her after seeing her.

Rushing her steps, Margo could have sworn that it took her only two seconds from the street to her front porch. She was about to press the doorbell when her mischievous mind suggested that she take Grey by surprise instead. Her husband was always conscious of securing the house and she was sure that he had all doors and windows locked already.

Margo hadn't been home for two days. Her new company was beginning to take too much of her time, and she wasn't the least happy that it would have to continue this way until McAmzee expanded its staff and shareholdings because of the new break. Margo took her work out her head and focused on finding the spare key in her bag instead. Luckily, she didn't have to search her bag for long before she found it.

Margo silently slid into the house with her blood rushing with excitement. Surprisingly, the television was on and the whole room brightened with the light from it. She could see the structure of their sitting room and was surprised that the sight seemed all new and pleasing to her. Her small flower pot was still beside the fire place and the flower glistened green with the light from the television. The light somehow made the red cushions appear like ghost apparition, giving the whole room a chilling temperature.

Grey himself was fast asleep on the couch that faced the television. His blond hair was the first part of his body that brought a brief smile on Margo's lips. She liked the fact that at his age, his hairs were still intact and his face only had a few wrinkles at his forehead and beside his nose. Grey hardly stressed himself and he loved drinking a lot. Margo constantly assumed that this helped his ageing in one way or the other.

She dropped her bag on another couch and approached the sleeping figure of her husband. She brushed a strand of his hair and watched with delight as his breaths became more even. He opened his eyes slightly and smiled up at her.

"Margo?" He whispered.

"Hi you." Margo whispered back at him.

He rested his face in her palm and closed his eyes briefly.

"I missed you." He whispered again.

I missed you more.

Margo didn't say the words. She went to the television and switched it off, allowing only the dimmed light from the dinning to partially illuminate the sitting room.

"Grey." She called, walking towards the three-seat couch beside the fireplace.

"Yes." Grey replied sleepily. There was a soft roughening sound as he stood from the couch.

"I am home." Margo started.

Then, her hands went to the zip of her long office skirt before she dragged the smooth material down her legs.

"And I want you." She told her husband.

She confirmed it that he also wanted her the moment she heard him groan in the darkness.

"He had been waiting the whole evening for me." She told herself.

When his fingers found her in the dark, Margo closed her eyes and enjoyed the waves of pleasure that reeked throughout her whole body. Grey began to unbutton her shirt after a while, and Margo simply stood there, expecting the dark room to be filled with the sweet sounds of her moans in the next few minutes.

But Margo finally told herself that she was expecting too much from her husband.

Grey was no longer the sex stud that he was when she married him. Or perhaps, Margo thought, it was her who no longer got sated with the few minutes that he spent whenever he made love to her. These days, she wanted more than Grey's touch or his soft whispers into her ears. It was as if her sexual fantasies had taken a whole new turn of wildness and adventure. Grey seemed to be unripe for the height of her sexual interest now, and Margo hoped to God that she wasn't losing her mind; or her love for her husband yet.

Margo Lattisaw might have doubted so many things in her life, but at the moment, as her husband finally had her entire clothes lying free on the floor and gently led her to a single couch in the center of the living room, Margo was sure about one thing:

She had reached a height of sexual resurgence that her husband could no longer handle or satisfy.

As if she needed the confirmation, she noticed that she couldn't feel the expected pleasure as Grey buried his hardness inside her. For him, it ended as fast as possible and he had rolled over to the bed, smiling and groaning as the shortened pleasure for her became his own fulfillment.

Margo almost cried out with irritation as Grey began to snore happily a few minutes later.

He was satisfied.

She was not.

And Margo Lattisaw began to move her own fingers into the wet clit between her thighs to make the want go away. A few seconds later, the whole room was filled with a round of soft whimper that accompanied the reverberating body of Margo, and she was so glad that her husband kept mourning, unaware of the changes that she had gone through.

Margo finally realized that she never needed Grey to satisfy herself. She could always take care of things herself.

Or look for another man who would.

C HAPTER O NE

The Chain Saw

Wincoston Lane was perhaps the most important dark alley in Tropical city. During the day, the alley was filled with countless happy faces and smiling new brides who were majorly seen to visit the various colorful and flower-adorned bridal shops that went down the short street. It was curious however how the bridal shops and its beautiful fun-filled corners became the dark alley during the night. When it was evening time, the bridal shops are closed and there were no longer candescent lights from the shops that filled up the lane. This alternatively keeps the lane dark and eerie afterwards; a remarkable change from the warm welcoming sight that it was during the day.

This remarkable change wasn't what made Wincostin Lane quite popular among folks in the city. No one could be so sure but the lane became quite famous after The Chain Saw became open more than ten years ago. The Chain Saw ran most of its operations during the night and was known to keep its night activities especially discreet and welcomed to members and constant lucky visitors only.

You only need buy a nice scorching bourbon drink from The Chain Saw's bar and ask for a very nice place to be entertained while you gorged the entire drink. The bartenders, a bunch of always-mischievous-looking characters, would then point to an almost invisible dark corner with a boring looking curtain. This curtain hid stairs behind it that led to a much more interesting night club below.

This night club was simply named "Saw". Every night, the host of the remarkable night club would explain with vigorous excitement the pun in the name "Chain Saw." He was simply called Teacake and he was a tall and muscled tattooed black man that always wore V-neck shirts that simply exposed his wide and rounded-breast chest to women who were always glad to cheer at it.

This night, Margo Lattisaw watched with gay interest as Teacake explained to the happy club attendees once again that the bar above was only the chain that led to the club below. It was the typical opening speech before things became overtly crazy and buzzing with uncontrollable sinful lust.

"You only need be wise and get to the chain before you find the saw!" Teacake screamed into the bustling speakers.

Immediately, the silent club buzzed with excitement as the whole light suddenly went out and immediately got replaced with infrared rays of green, blue and red lights that made it seems as if everyone's body glowed with inexplicable lusty aura. It was awesome and what came next after this always got to Margo.

Immediately, a center stage was created at the middle of Saw's dancing hall and Teacake was at the center of attraction once again. His voice cracked this time around as he introduced new strippers to his ever attentive audience.

"And introducing…….the bestial pound of hard, sultry, incomparably evil and complete naked and solid male flesh….I introduce to you…." Teacake was good at the introductions, and this time around, he paused for the effect before he finally pointed out the fourth stripper for the day.

"Oh oh, I have heard that women bury their own fingers in the soft flesh of their own palms just at the sight of this one." Teacake announced. "Well, I think they should for here is a sight that would get your tits buzzing hard with excitement! I introduce to you tonight the unforgiving 'Beast'!"

Teacake was certainly good at introductions and it wasn't always long before Teacake wowed everyone with presentations of blazingly sexy and half naked men who all held one sex toy or common items wrapped in polythene that interested the audience the most.

This time around, Teacake introduced four grown and wondrously beautiful men that weren't too shy to get to work already. Teacake, as usual, disappeared amongst the crowd and there were the strippers on stage gradually taking most attention that the cheerful host soon became a forgotten memory.

It wasn't Margo's first time at The Chain Saw and it wasn't the first time that she was allowing herself a good time staring at handsome young men either. They satisfied her own curiosity with their presence on stage and the various mode that most of them played while they virtually took off all their clothes. At the moment, the fourth character was already causing responsive whimpers and shrieks from the crowd of female clubbers as he slowly took off his shirt to reveal truly blazing hot and sexy upper body that housed nice abs and wide chest.

It wasn't what he was doing but Margo found herself leaning forward to have a better l0ok. She wasn't just any customer in Saw, so she had a very cozy corner at a round balcony above the dancing hall for herself alone and for any stripper that caught her fancy. At the moment, that "pound of male flesh" caught even more than her fancy as he unrolled the polythene that was in his hand and turned the object over his head. Immediately, his whole body was filled with liquid substance that appeared like blood.

"Oh my!" Margo whispered from her VIP corner.

The stripper's leggings was a very thin material and the lines that immediately appeared between his thighs were suggestive and impressive enough. He must have planned the transparency of his huge manhood though, for the stripper was now touching his own naked body from the curls of his hair and towards the tiny lace of thin hair that went from his abdomen downwards towards the wider area beneath his leggings. A particular woman yelped with extreme pleasure as the stripper held the hem of his leggings, ready to draw them down.

It was after the leggings was down and another thin and shorter tight was exposed around the strippers thigh that Margo realized that the whimper was her own voice. She could no longer take the teasing sight of the stripper from the balcony. She wanted him in front of her, while the curtains of the corner blocked the rest of the club from them.

"I want him to touch me and make me more than whimper." Margo unashamedly confessed to herself.

Having thought enough, Margo closed her eyes, took a few short breaths and signaled one of the club attendants to move closer.

"Tell Teacake I would have a word." She whispered above the loud music.

When the attendant nodded meekly and scurried off to get Teacake, Margie knew it was done.

Soon, whoever that stripper was, she was going to have him to herself for the rest of the night.

And then, she was going to make the beast hers.

"How about you tell me more about yourself, Xavier, besides the fact that you are twenty-two?" Margo suddenly asked the young stud.

It was the second time that Margo was meeting with the young stripper after that night at Saw and for every new second that she spent with the restless cougar, she was beginning to think that meeting him was going to be permanently what she does everyday now. Xavier was certainly a professional stripper who was better with stripping women's clothing. She was presently naked to the toes and was gradually accepting the fact that she had had sex three times already with another man in a cheap outskirt hotel and it beats having sex with Grey in their home for more than six years now.

"You want to know about me?" Xavier asked. He seemed surprised.

Margo managed to smile at him before she answered him.

"Of course. I am curious."

She knew she really shouldn't have pushed the topic but Xavier seemed like a young man who wouldn't talk about himself. She was indeed curious about the kind of life that he lived. She was sure that he lived a dangerously reckless life and probably had a room somewhere in the city stashed with weed. He has a blue angel wing tattooed at his back and Margo was already betting that it was the sign of some street gang.

However, Xavier shocked Margo when he shifted his body on the bed and started talking about college.

"Well, if you insist. I currently attend classes on Investment Banking at the City College." Xavier rested his head on both palms and was staring straight into Margo'e eyes.

This made it almost impossible to hide her shock, and Margo had to force a smile to make him more comfortable. If he noticed that her eyes fluttered immediately with surprise though, Xavier didn't show it. He continued and expressed how much it was stressful to work part time and still attend classes.

"Well, I made arrangement for convenient times for classes but it isn't always easy running through school work, work at Saw and during the day, full-time work at the local Walmart. I sometimes could not hide the fatigue."

Fatigue? Margo almost found it hard to believe that a man who could lay her on her back thrice in one night was fatigued before even starting.

"Did you say local Walmart?" Margo asked, wondering how he did it.

"Does old lady Whitmore pay you well?" She added when Xavier's eyebrow raised with confusion.

"Well, dear old Mrs. Whitmore is a very nice and compassionate boss, if that answers the question." Xavier replied cooly.

Nice and compassionate?

Margo suddenly felt as if there was something that Xavier wasn't telling her. Meanwhile, she was already accepting that she was subsequently getting jealous of Xavier spending most of the day with the other woman instead.

"How about I give you double what you earn at Whitmore's and you stop working for her?" Margo suddenly chirped.

It took almost two seconds before Xavier said or did anything. He rose from the bed first and stood completely naked, with his arms folded across his chest. His erect penis stood tall and was facing Margo with a stern.

Doesn't it get tired!

Margo raised her head and managed to focus on the expression on Xavier instead. He seemed to have gotten more confused with her recent question.

"I ain't complaining about my current job, Margo." He advanced.

Margo wasn't sure she held out her hand to show a bit of compassion or because her hands wanted to circle around the thickness of his already aroused manhood. The solid flesh shot out harder as

Xavier stared at her, a lot of questions in his head.

"And I ain't complaining about your current job sugar." Margo imitated his African-American accent.

She began to move her hands up and down, watching with interest as the sensitive flesh in her hands responded by getting harder and bigger.

"Margo?" Xavier's young voice called out.

"Careful dear, you might get it shy." Margo teased, getting his lips paused before he said anything else.

"So, this is what you are going to do." Margo started, moving her head towards the tip of his hardness.

She swallowed his dick whole and smiled when he groaned with delight. No matter, Xavier loved her touching him the same way she dreamt about his dick inside her every counting seconds at work.

"What?" He managed to say between clenched teeth.

Margo almost forgot that she was getting him to agree to something before.

"You stop working for old and dear lady Whitmore and spend the time with me instead – wherever and whenever I need you. I pay you triple then." Margo dropped both hands from Xavier's fully aroused dick and looked up at him, waiting.

As calculated, he looked down at her as if his heart had been ripped from his heart and he was dying. It almost delighted her heart with too much blood rush to see him hold her hands and return them back to his dick.

"Whenever and wherever?" He asked.

Margo didn't respond to this. She knew he had no choice now.

And with the way that Xavier was moving towards her and further on the bed, Margo knew she had no choice at the moment too.

The night wasn't over yet. And Xavier sure wasn't through fucking her.

CHAPTER TWO

Daydreaming

"Mrs. Lattisaw?"

Margo jolted out of her imagination as her name sounded in her ears the second time. Gradually, she realized that she was inattentively biting the edge of her pencil and was staring into an empty space in her office. The printer beside her had stopped printing the document she started a while ago and was beeping red, signaling that there were no longer papers in the tray.

"Mrs. Lattisaw?"

It was Pete, her new secretary and he was staring at her as if she had completely lost it.

"Yes, what do you want, Pete?"

Margo waved him in from the door that he was so afraid to step through. He seemed as if he was about to say something when he stopped in front of her desk, but his face fell to the floor instead. He quickly dropped the files in his hands on the table and rushed through the description of what he has for her.

"You have a long list of call logs you haven't attended to Mrs. Lattisaw. Your husband called a few times already, requesting that you called him and let him know if you were coming home after all."

Pete paused for a while, and Margo couldn't but noticed that a wrinkle was already forming around Pete's cheeks. Pete, if Margo remembered correctly, celebrated his fortieth birthday the year before.

"And Mr. Simons asked if he could get an appointment with you tomorrow." Pete was still reporting.

"Well, is he going to meet me again and beg to do anything just to have me employ him back and give him another chance?" Margo cut him short.

"Well, the other staff would agree that you should." Pete softly chirped in.

Margo knew Pete was perhaps the only member of staff who was honest with her. And she also knew that there was some staff who thought that she was being too harsh with Simons. Whereas, Simons had almost ruined the company when he almost classified secrets on the total description of the new asthma drug to one of his lovers who worked for another pharmaceutical company.

"The result of compelling bed talks." The idiot of a man had the gut to given as an excuse.

"Well, 'the other staff' wouldn't know how unemployed all of them would have been had I not been trailing Simons' recent activity and with a woman that made him too occupied to come to work." Margo told Pete.

Unfortunately, explaining issues surrounding Simons at the moment was making it impossible to think of Xavier or her husband, Grey. She wasn't ashamed though that she was doing everything possible to satisfy her sexual urges and that includes spending more time with her sex toy, Xavier and the littlest time with Grey.

"Well, should I fix the appointment?" Pete asked.

"I would rather you shouldn't." Margo quickly instructed.

She was now checking the files that Pete had dropped on her table and glanced up at Pete. His head was still facing the floor and it was almost impossible not to notice that he was uncomfortable being in the office with her.

"Well, Pete, you want me to read these and call you back here if I don't get the briefings at all?" She asked, curious about Pete's unusual coyness.

It was as if Pete was waiting for the question. He nodded his head and almost had it off his neck with the rigorous shake. Then, he scurried to the door, allowing Margo to open the first document that read "Call Logs."

"Mrs. Lattisaw?" Pete wasn't gone yet.

"Yes   Pete?"   Margo   asked, expecting   that   he   was   about   to announce   a   report   that   he   had probably forgotten to include in the files.

"That's a nice T-shirt. I forgot to mention." He simply stated.

"Oh thanks Pete." Margo managed to say before Pete disappeared behind the door.

She dropped the file in her hands and dropped her gaze to check the shirt that she was wearing. Her smile froze almost immediately.

"Oh!" Margo gasped.

She finally understood why Pete was inexcusably uncomfortable staring at her from across the table. She buried her face in her palms with shame as she realized what had happened.

Somehow, while she ran the printer and started thinking about what she had in plan for tonight's adventure with Xavier, she had unlaced the top of her chest and her full breast was visible for everyone to see.

Poor Pete probably couldn't find the strength to stop staring at them.

Her cheeks flushing with heat, Margo began lacing her shirt.

She realized that she wasn't really ashamed; instead she could feel her nipple tighten with the excitement that at her age, her fair skinned breasts could still get anyone uncomfortable.

❖

It took almost an hour before Margo finally found the unhealthy neighborhood that Teacake described to be totally unfit for someone of her status. Instead, horny and in need of Xavier alone, Margo had stubbornly refused the man's advice and had set out to find Xavier. She had promised herself that she was going to hang on to his naked body wherever she met him and make him make love to her even, even if it was at the end of a sewer. Unfortunately, that decision was weakening every moment that she drove silently through the street that was described for her.

It was late in the evening already and it was almost impossible to distinguish if it was still evening or it was night already. Xavier doesn't leave in the neighborhood but Teacake had described it as the only place to find Xavier whenever he disappeared and wasn't picking his calls.

Margo had been worried sick for the past two days when he stopped picking his calls. Surprisingly, she had pushed herself to ask lady Whitmore if she had seen him around but the old woman had only rolled her eyes and mentioned that Xavier must have rolled away with a fine corny bitch who would drive him nuts and unsuccessful afterwards. It took mostly her self-control not to scream at lady Whitmore that Xavier had no woman, nor bitch, but herself.

But then, after leaving the Walmart, Margo had headed to Saw with the memory of the previous nights with Xavier replaying in her head. Now, that she was driving through the street that had been described to her at Saw, the memory was coming back again, making driving or seeing the street before her quite difficult.

Xavier had taken her to his home instead a few nights ago. Surprisingly, his room was rather exotic and finely painted and furnished. He had numerous and impressive flowerpots which filled the better part of his room apartment. Apart from the richly carved flower pots, there were also good taste paintings on the wall, and it was as if he was the one that drew some of the small ones that he hung in the little corner that he set aside as his dinning.

"I wouldn't think that young men these days still quite buy into good picture and sculpture taste." Margo commented when she stopped studying his room.

"Well, I did end up with you." Xavier commented too.

"You think being with me is good taste?" Margo teased him back.

He smiled childishly at her and started moving towards the bed.

"Well, how about you get over here and tell me what to do to answer that question."

Margo remembered the excitement that she felt between her thighs when heard those words. For over two weeks now, Xavier was the perfect man that made sex quite interesting, fulfilling and tiring at the same time. He was gradually driving her nuts!

She had trailed behind him to the bed and then watched as he sat at the edge of the bed and faced her.

"Taste is a matter of perspective after activity I have heard." He whispered.

Margo wasn't sure she understood what he was saying but she knew she had an idea of what she was going to make him do already. And God helping, he was in the right position already.

"How about you tell me what you see when you look at me?" She asked him, already making a move that was soon going to get him aroused for her in a while.

The question surprised Xavier though but he quickly hid the surprise between a shy but wide smile. His hand went for her waist as she approached him before he spoke.

"Well, dear compelling Margo. All I see is a very attractive woman who regardless of her growing age is perhaps the most seductive and magnetic female I have ever come across."

Xavier got the cue as she raised her folded her skirt to her waist until her thighs and everything above was available for his touch. His palms left her waist then and moved downwards. He began to move his palms across her thighs, adding to the heat down there.

"Now, moving on to when you are naked," Xavier continued, "I would like to think that you remind me of jam-filled doughnut with chocolate fillings and a cup of lemonade on the tray with it. You are exotic and wonderful woman."

Margo had to laugh and moan at the same time as his words and fingers worked magic on her at the same time. Xavier would have passed for the most intoxicating and addicting lover for any woman. He was just irresistible and it was actually terrible that he knew that he was.

"Appropriate words." She told him, impressed with what he was doing at her thighs already.

He started by pushing down her panties and finally exposing her wet clit to full view. He smiled briefly up at her before he began to trace gentle line across the soft mound of flesh that surrounded the area. Then, in a flash, the index finger slid fast into her, causing an unexpected gasp to let loose from her throat.

"You like that?" He asked, and didn't wait for her to answer before he doubled the finger and pushed in faster.

"Xavier!"

He seemed to have been aggravated with the mention of his name on her lips. He withdrew both finger again and pressed back into her clit with a renewed maddening stroke.

"Xavier!" Margo called out again.

Her whole body reverberated with want and lust, and anticipation. She knew that he was aware of what she wanted. Like the beast that he was, he was only killing her first, before giving her the pleasure that she wanted.

His fingers were now pushing harder and faster into her clit, rendering her knees weaker every moment. The only way she thought that she could control her failing body was to keep calling his name. This time around, Margo buried her fingers in his curly hair and dragged him closer.

"Xavier!" She cried out again.

It was the last time she did before she felt his tongue first on her clit before he took everything in his mouth. A few minutes later, Xavier was having his mouth everywhere and she was just screaming with delight and extreme ecstasy. She wondered why she survived his mouth or the force of his hard dick when he got up in a flash and pushed it inside her like a famished lion in a cage.

Sometimes, Margo forgets that she was above fifty and Xavier was only a young man in his twenties. He was fast, always ready and sometimes forgot to handle her with care. Fortunately, Margo never wanted him to handle her with care. She wouldn't have opted into a relationship with a renowned scandalous male stripper if she wanted to be handled like a fragile old lady. She needed sex; raw, fast, soulful and scandalous.

"Well, driving in this Godforsaken neighborhood is scandalous, Margo." Margo finally found the sane words to convince her that she wasn't thinking straight.

She jolted out of the memory of her past activities with Xavier and focused on why she was driving further into a seemingly ghetto street just to look for her sugar boy. Of course, she needed him at the moment but it wasn't worth the stare that she was getting from the folks as she drove past. A particular group of younger men had stopped playing dice at the porch of an abandoned house as she drove and whistled mischievously at her car.

"Hey money mama!" One of them cried out.

"You looking for us!" Another cooed.

It wasn't until Margo found an almost empty space to park that she stopped driving. It wasn't as if the place wasn't filled with odd looking men and women also but it had other cars parked in the area as well, and the house that was described to her was sitting across the parking space.

"You should see get schoolboy Xavier there anytime." Teacake had murmured. "And tell the young bastard he is reducing my customers! He should show up tonight or he ain't ever gonna get paid!"

It wasn't until Teacake mentioned that Xavier hadn't been showing up at the night club too that Margo had decided to go looking for him. But thinking about Teacake's threat that Xavier wouldn't be paid, she doubt it that would move him. She now paid her cupcake sweet boy enough money to pay his fees at school and to forget working at the Walmart. His only work for almost one month now was to make her feel good, or simply put, make her moan and groan her brains out whenever she needed him.

"So, where the hell was he now?" Margo frustratingly whispered as she got out of the car.

She quickly adjusted her hat and placed the dark shades beautifully across her eyes. Luckily for her, the sun was blazing hot and shinning bright during the day and no one would suspect that she was only trying to hide her face. Again, another group of young men whistled as she scurried by and walked towards the front porch of the small bungalow that had been described to her. The bungalow looked surprisingly small but kempt. There were no flowers in front of it, but the painting was better than the rest of the house on the street and the windows, unlike other windows on the street had its louvers unbroken and well cleaned and dusted. If Margo didn't know better, she would have thought that Xavier hired someone always to help him take care of the house or perhaps, this was his mother's home.

If it was the former, Margo began to wonder what Xavier wanted alone in such a dangerous looking environment. She didn't want to think about him again as she had first thought that he was a crook with a bag of drugs stashed somewhere. So far, Xavier had proven to her that he was hell bent on becoming an investment banker and not even all the women in Saw would distract him from his goal.

Margo finally built up the nerve to forget about the trail of eyes that had followed her to the front porch. She adjusted her shades and tapped gently on the door. She didn't have to tap it twice before she heard Xavier's deep voice. She couldn't hear what he was saying but it was definitely obvious that he wasn't the only one in the house.

"Margo!" Xavier exclaimed as he opened the door.

Margo removed her shades and was ready to rebuke him for disappearing in a while without informing her. But then, she noticed that he didn't exclaim because he was delighted to see her. He did because he wasn't happy to. The emotions on his face quickly betrayed him.

"What are you doing here?" He quickly asked, stepping on the porch and closing the door behind him.

Margo couldn't believe that he was behaving as if she had no right to come looking at him. She almost pointed it out to him that he was perhaps the most ungrateful and uncouth young man there is on the streets. She had been worried sick that he was wounded somewhere or maybe he was in trouble. All the while, he had been up to God-knows-what in the middle of nowhere. And he was now whispering at her as if there really was something that he was up to.

"I should be asking you, Xavier, what you are doing here!" Margo literally had to look round at the vicinity of the house for the right effect. It wasn't a place where she really should park her car or walk into. Surprisingly, the men and women around were now facing their business. No one stared at her or Xavier.

"Well, I come here sometimes to chill, overprotective sugar mama!" Xavier rolled his eyes, but not before she landed her palm on his cheek.

"Call me that one more time you uncouth child and you might have somewhere else that you might want to chill in for the next three days."

It wasn't the right words to threaten him but her face expressed everything. Xavier seemed to be controlling his confusion, the attraction he has for her and his anger all at the same time. His breath wasn't normal for a while but then, his gaze dropped to the floor and Margo couldn't believe that she silently chided herself that she had overreacted.

"What have you been doing here, Xavier?" She spoke

compassionately now, reaching out to touch the spot that she had hit him.

"He came here to be with me." A female's voice suddenly answered from behind Xavier.

Margo had to turn her head in order to view the younger girl that stood confidently at the door behind Xavier. She was wearing only her underwear – a color blend of a red lace bra and a very thin-layered pant that plastered against the thinness of her waist and her round buttocks. Margo quickly assessed her and concluded that she was perhaps a year younger than Xavier and worked out quite often. She had a die-for body for someone her age.

"And who…."Margo had to stop the question before she finished it.

She ran a mental calculation in her head and came out with the idea that the only reason Xavier was awfully quiet and secretive was because he was having an affair. And he had the gut to ignore her calls for almost three days.

"Care to tell me what is going on here, boy?" Margo asked instead. She was boiling hot with some jealousy temperament.

Surprisingly, Xavier managed to keep his cool. He walked over to the younger girl at the door and stood beside her, folding his arms across his chest the same way he did whenever he was trying to prove a point or build up his confidence.

"This is Alexus, Margo."

Xavier dropped both hands and clutched Alexus' fingers with his.

"She is my girlfriend."

Whatever sexual feeling Margo must have been feeling before she came to the bungalow, it vaporized immediately after listening to Xavier's words. She could no longer think of anything except the fact that Xavier had just made the biggest mistake of his life. He was trying to smile at her but she knew that a lot was going on in his head as well. Alexus on the other hand was staring at Margo as if she was some shameful woman that needed to get her bearings.

Margo wasn't surprised that Alexus hadn't even wanted to know who she was. She guessed that her kinds only cared about what they wanted, and by the look of where she was living, Margo also guessed that she wasn't the kind of woman that left anything of hers for the grab. Well, Margo thought, Xavier was hers for a month and things weren't going to stop just because he came across some spoilt bitchy slim waist that looked too gorgeous to be true.

Xavier was her boy toy and she had grown some inexplicable feelings towards him over the past few weeks. She dreamt of him every hour of the day and this was perhaps the best experience she had ever felt all her life.

Not even his pretty girlfriend was going to take those feelings away from her.

CHAPTER THREE

Underdog

Margo sighed heavily as she stepped into the familiar warmness of her large four-bedroom duplex house. As usual, the first item her gaze fell on was the flowerpot that was beside the fireplace. It wasn't entirely night time yet but the whole house seemed dark except from the small glow that came from the table lamp that was on the stool near the dinning.

Margo noticed that Grey wasn't in the sitting room as the television was off too. Recently, the fireplace had received no burning woods since she summer had come with full force and everywhere had been virtually hot. But this wasn't why the house was quite dull and lifeless, Margo thought. It was because Grey was the only one at home mostly and she had just abandoned him to fend for her own sexual needs; not that she regretted it yet though.

Margo thought about what had happened with Xavier earlier in the day and had to admit that the continuous thought of him and Alexus was exhausting her. She had done nothing but walk away after Xavier introduced Alexus as his girlfriend. She didn't know why, but something had paralyzed her, especially when she found out that knowing that Xavier was with another woman hurt her in such an inexplicable way.

"What is wrong with me?" Margo whispered, unable to see anything as her eyes filled with tears.

She knew that things weren't so simple with her needs and her relationship with her husband in the past few days. In fact, she knew that Grey suspected that some things were wrong with her, but he was the ever-patient man who always cared too much about her. Unfortunately, he wasn't seeing the change in her. She now avoided talking to him or even making love to him.

Now, the only man that filled that sexual lust was with another girl, and the funny thing was that Xavier hadn't even ran after her as she left angrily. His ungrateful ass had stayed rooted at the porch with his spoilt brat girl the whole time until she drove speedily off.

"Fuck!" Margo shrieked.

She stood up suddenly and turned towards the room upstairs. She needed someone to talk to and Grey suddenly felt like the only man that could calm her down. She could only think of all the years that she had spent talking to him about everything until the past few years. Grey had changed suddenly before she did. First, he had started extreme drinking and then, his sexual prowess had reduced.

Thrice or four times in a week now, Grey was drunk and chattered nonsense in the house. At first, she had blamed herself for not looking out for him after he retired at his property development work almost four years ago. Now, he was always at the retail office, and when he was alone at home, he was getting himself drunk before she was back. But then, Margo was growing older too and he wasn't even available to look out for her as well. Margo reminded herself that she had never been the strong woman who took care of things. She was fragile and successful without excuse.

"Grey?" Margo called out as she took the stairs to the small bar that was at the study.

She knew where Grey would be if he wasn't in front of the television. He drank or read throughout the afternoon and it was usually a sore to the eye to see him wasted and weak during the night. He was no longer living his life right.

"Here." Grey whispered as she stepped into the study.

He looked tired and exhausted as he tried to move towards her from the bar. Unable to move further, he stopped moving and fell on the armchair.

"I am tired, Margo." He muttered.

Margo walked towards her husband and began to smoothen his hair with her palm. She knew he wasn't fit to listen to her the same way he did over the years that they were married. She could only rely on her own method for now.

"Just sleep sweetie." She whispered into his ears.

He smiled briefly and then his breath became even as he drifted off to sleep. After a while, Margo noticed that he was now snoring too.

She collected the glass cup in his hands and returned it to the bar, clearing the tiles. If there was anything that made Margo sad these days, it was having to come back home some times and meet

Grey sprawled on the floor or on a chair after he had drank too much. It made him different from the man that she once knew and *it also made meeting with another man outside easier.*

Margo shook her head as she battled with the idea that Grey's drinking habit was what drove her out into night clubs. While this is partially true, she was also ready to accept that it was out of her own curiosity. She suddenly wanted more than the satisfaction that her husband could deliver, and here she was, lonely and sad after wasting her money and fully satisfying herself with weekend and weekdays debauchery with the stripper cougar.

But was she truly satisfied or was she thinking of backing down because of a young street girl that looked too tough to be dealt with?

Margo suddenly found herself pouring herself a drink. She just needed the liquid to burn her throat and reminded her that she was still in control of her life. She had a sex drive that needed to be calmed and only Xavier could do that.

Then why was she drinking instead of thinking of a way to get her toy boy back?

She brought the cup to her lips and closed her eyes as the scotch expectedly burnt her throat and slid energetically to her stomach. When she opened her eyes, Margo suddenly felt as if things were going to get better. She took the bottle with her and exited the study, refusing to look at the sleeping figure of her husband on the armchair.

Suddenly energized and thinking straight, Margo advanced towards the sitting room and reached for her phone in her silk skirt pocket. She dialed Simons' number and listened as a soft beep came up almost immediately after the first ring.

"Margo? Boy, am I so glad that you finally decided to call me." Simon's rough voice came up.

"I haven't forgiven you yet." She told him.

He sighed softly before he said anything into the phone.

"I want in back, Maggie." He whispered.

Apart from being her employee, Simons was Margo's childhood friend and the only person that called her Maggie. She wouldn't have been so angry at him for almost selling the company out had they not been so close.

"I would do anything to be back, Maggie." Simons was saying again.

His words were going along with what she was about to ask him.

"Anything?" She handled the phone with her other hand and reached for a pen in her bag after she began to doubt something in her head.

"Yes, anything! I worked so hard for years to perfect that drug with you and you know it! So, anything!" Simons seemed excited that Margo was finally thinking of having him back.

"Well, there is one thing that I want you to do." Margo finally let the words out.

She looked at the paper that she quickly scribbled on as Simons spoke through the phone. She still remembered the address correctly after all, she told herself.

"Anything." Simons repeated.

"Do you by chance still have the right connections with the underdogs?" She asked Simons.

The line went silent for a while and Margo almost thought that Simons had dropped the call. But she could still hear his soft breaths and waited patiently for him to reply her.

"Woman! I am the underdog!" He rasped into the phone.

Good.

"Perfect." Margo whispered into the phone.

She read out the address that she had written down to her childhood friend and told him everything that she needed him to do.

She was getting Xavier back by all cost.

❖

"What have you done!"

Xavier was hurrying towards her at her VIP corner in Saw. As expected, the two bouncers that Teacake gave her whenever she visited blocked his passage as he neared and he looked on at her, expecting some special treatment.

"You can shout at me from there, Xavier." She told him, not taking her eyes from the interesting view downstairs.

Xavier seemed helpless as he stared on, unable to do anything but cower before the heavily built black men that blocked his movement towards her. His face finally pleaded before he spoke.

"I wasn't shouting." He whispered.

Margo finally looked up into his face and smiled at both bouncers. She tapped her fingers and signaled that they should let him into her solitary sexual den. Her VIP corner had a long and wide couch that was sprayed with blue and red flowers with overwhelming summer fragrance. Sitting there alone made her horny before she entertained herself with the performance of the strippers downstairs.

"So, the toy boy returns to the sugar mama." Margo teased, unable to keep the laughter.

"Alexus doesn't take weed and you know it." Xavier whispered, pleading.

"I do not know anything about the women that you cheat with, impetuous you." Margo chided.

But she knew very well that Alexus had just been recently taken in by the cops after a very efficient tip miraculously came on at the local police that a young attractive woman was keeping a sack of white and brown substance for some unknown gunmen in her house. The tip had been so wise to supply the girl's address as well.

Margo glanced sideways at Xavier as he sat beside her, reaching out for her hand. He kissed her sensitive palm and looked up at her.

"If you put her there, then you can get her out?" He asked, refusing to believe that Margo had nothing to do about the stashed weed.

Margo knew that she was always weak to Xavier's touch and looks. He was pleading with those eyes, but unknown to him, he was also making her thighs weak and wanting his touch. She wanted him to undress himself as soon as possible and go about the hell of everything that she paid him to do. He was her stripper. Her boy. Hers alone.

"Yes, I can." She told him.

"I promise to forget everything about her if you would, mi amor. I would behave."

Oh, he speaks Latin now?

Every second that passed by with Xavier pleading for her mercy, Margo wanted him the more. She realized that she would be forever weak to his boyish whims, especially his irresistible touch. His fingers had left her fingers and were now gradually moving towards her breasts. He nipples already tickled hard with excitement.

"Deal." Margo accepted, unable to keep herself from touching him.

From his words, she knew that he was swearing his loyalty to her, even though it was only to get Alexus out of prison. It doesn't matter why he was doing it, Margo told herself. What really mattered was that the only man that made her feel completely lustful was virtually begging her right now, and she was going to tell him everything would be okay between them now.

She welcomed Xavier back by dragging him closer and whistling to the bouncers who stood watchful at the entrance of the VIP corner. Immediately, the blind curtain came down and it was only her and Xavier sighing as hands began to hit on clips of clothes and buttons of shirts. Immediately, Xavier was in action and he had totally stripped her coat over her head, revealing her naked breasts.

"I never quite understand how you keep this twins floated and round."

He teased, before he brought his head towards the tip of one breast.

Margo smiled satisfactorily as his lips paused on a nipple before he started suckling it. She told herself that she missed his warm mouth teasing the tiny buds of her nipples as well.

"You are mine now." She whispered, unable to breathe evenly as he suckled on.

As if Xavier agreed with her, he guided her towards the soft cushion of the couch and placed himself on her. He didn't even bother to strip her of her skirt or panties. He simply folded the skirt above her hips, shifted the thin material of her panties to the side to expose her clit, and drove his hard dick in fast.

"You are mine." Margo whispered again.

She wanted this to go on forever.

CHAPTER FOUR

Terror

Margo finished frying her evening bacon and was about to set it with a cold milk drink on a stool when a soft rasp came on the door. She smiled and rushed back to the kitchen to wipe her hands on a napkin, happy that Grey was back so early.

It was just six and Grey usually wasn't back until seven or quarter past six. Either ways, he was home early these days and she hardly thought he was drinking heavily as he did before. Something was different about everyone these past few weeks and it was almost awkward that every beautiful day was getting things better and better.

Grey hadn't totally stopped drinking but he minimized his everyday stupor to just a glass fill of scotch or bourbon. Meanwhile, he started talking about getting back on his feet and it was almost impossible to believe when Margo came home to meet his entire beards and hair all trimmed neat. It was as if Grey could see something that she wasn't seeing. He wanted to keep living.

Meanwhile, for two weeks now, Xavier attended the new session at college and hasn't even said any word on Alexus since the cops let her out. He has resumed his performance as the Beast at Saw and wasn't even wasting any time when it came to sexually satisfying her. Margo wouldn't have wished for a better week, no matter how awkward things had turned.

At McAvee too, the Ozone had finally hit the market and everything was going profitably well as planned. Surprisingly, having Simons back was the right move since he wasn't always afraid to get his hands dirty with sales schmicks. She had to put him in charge of all stock and trade options and he was quite good at it.

She let go of these thoughts as she advanced to unlock the door for

Grey. She couldn't explain it, but these days, she was always anxious to see her husband every day. It was as if she was regaining the loving spirit that she had for him before, or the curiosity that made her think of him panting hard above her whenever she came back from work. Everything was rushing back to her in the past few days. Things couldn't have been more awkward, she told herself again.

As Margo finally opened the door, she told herself that the sight of the gun that greeted her wasn't what she had expected to end the awkwardness that filled the days that went by. At her front porch was Alexus Jenkins and she sure wasn't paying a courtesy visit.

❖

Her eyes burned with anger and vengeance as she pointed the gun at Margo's chest. She was staring sparingly at the objects in the house but it was obvious that a little movement from Margo could be dangerous.

Margo sat patiently on the chair that Alexus had drawn out for her after she had silently led her back into the house with the motion of the gun. Alexus seemed to have come for something, and it was obvious that she wasn't leaving until she got it. Or perhaps, *Alexus is here to just take my life*.

The young girl's gaze dropped on a frame on the wall and she finally concentrated on Margo.

"I had to find out myself that you were married." Alexus spat on the floor after she spoke. "He was fucking you for weeks and he didn't even want to know where you lived."

Margo wanted to explain that it was the kind of relationship that was safe for any secret couple, or for debaucheries such as theirs, but she couldn't. Any aggravation caused by her words could make Alexus make the biggest mistake of her life. Margo didn't even know where Xavier lived too. These were common things.

"Well, I want my man back." Alexus ranted.

This got on Margo's nerves.

"He isn't yours to take." She yelled back.

Surprisingly, this was funny to Alexus as her laughter reeked throughout the whole dinning.

"How old are you, Margo? Fifty-five?"

This shut Margo up. She didn't know why but Alexus' laughter suddenly felt like a ridicule.

"Fifty." Margo supplied.

In a flash, Alexus advanced with the gun and placed it at Margo's forehead. She has a hard time deciding whether she should pull the trigger or simply decided a better body part to shoot. She finally pulled the gun back up and stepped back. Margo realized that she had held her breath and closed her eyes the whole time.

"What do you want?" Margo asked, when it seemed as if Alexus hasn't decided what she was going to do with her yet.

"What do I want?"

Alexus seemed to be angered by this question. She reached for a small porcelain jug that was at the wall cupboard and threw it against the nearby wall.

"What do I want!" She shouted again, what I want is to ruin your life as you have mine." She finally said, smiling chivalrously.

Margo didn't understand what Alexus was ranting about. Yes, she had her arrested but it was only for a few hours, possibly a day, before Simons waved his magic wand and she was out again.

"I had only one chance with college and you blew it for me when you had me arrested!" Alexus shouted, raising the gun again at Margo.

Margo finally understood. She never really thought that a girl such as Alexus would be interested in going to college. Apparently, most major schools in the world hardly admit ex-convicts or children with constant arrest track record.

"You really shouldn't have gotten involved with Xavier." Margo confidently remarked.

She was getting tired of the child's sordid rants and remarks. She obviously wasn't in her home to kill her, or else she would be dead already.

Surprisingly, she was right. Alexus lowered her weapon but the fire and anger was still visible in her eyes. She kept Margo in her seat with a fiery glance that shoved fear into Margo's heart.

"What have you done?" Margo suddenly realized why Alexus was in her house.

Alexus laughed hysterically before she said anything. Her eyes tingled with mischief and it made Margo fear what was coming without even knowing it.

"Well, your husband would soon be back with a parcel that was dropped at his desk at the retail office, Margo. I am sure he would come home to recount the countless pictures of you and Xavier making love throughout the night at an infamous night club."

Margo could stop her eyes from widening with shock. She was totally unprepared for the next words that accompanied this news.

"You know, I am quite sure Xavier was tired of the milf sex between you two. It was why he sought me out. He sought me, Margo; he did. I didn't have to seduce his young mind with money or adult sex. I only had to make him feel young and alive. Apparently, that caught him faster than your old falling breasts."

Margo didn't want to believe everything that Alexus was saying but it all sounded like the truth. She was the only one who had lusted after Xavier. It never really happened that he came after her one time or twice because he simply wanted to fuck her. He had indeed been the sex toy and nothing more. He had no feelings towards her.

"And right now," Alexus already started moving towards the sitting room. "I just got the idea that news houses need those pictures too."

Alexus turned to look at her with another mischievous smile before she hid the gun in her skirt.

"it would make a good front page apart from the recent growth of your company that Mrs. Margo Lattisaw was fucking young student and part-time stripper, Xavier Keller." Alexus eventually said before turning towards the door.

"Hell no!" Margo yelled.

Margo couldn't explain the urgency or the hateful energy that took over her in an instant. As Alexus advanced towards the door, she reached immediately for the lamp at the dinning and ran after her. It didn't bother her that Alexus raised her hand in shock as she approached her or even bothered to reach for her gun underneath her top. Margo was fast enough and she was able to land the heavy metal handle of the lamp on the young girl's head.

At the same time, the sound of the gun went off and Margo couldn't but noticed that she staggered back in pain.

As she gazed down at the lifeless body of Alexus on the floor of the sitting room, Margo finally knelt on the floor with much effort and continued to stare as blood flowed from a part of Alexus' head to the rug on the floor. Just then, it seemed as if some persons were rushing from outside the house to get inside very quickly. Finally, the front door opened and two men stood there, shocked and awestruck by the spectacle before them.

"Grey?" Margo whispered.

"I am here." She could hear his voice as he ran to meet her.

As he held her into his arms, Margo could see his face clearly before she turned to look at the other man at the door. Xavier wasn't even attempting to move into the house. He started stepping backward before he finally turned and ran into the darkening urban street beyond.

"Careful sweet." Grey whispered beside her. "You are going to be fine."

She wanted to ask about Alexus but she was finding it hard to talk. Trying to shift her head to see Alexus' lifeless body again, she came face to face with the parcel that Alexus had claimed to have dropped in Grey's office. Grey had dropped the parcel on the floor as he bent to pick her up. Obviously, he had seen the content too, and there was no explaining how he and Xavier came home to her at the same time.

"Grey…." She tried to speak again.

"It's okay…." Grey whispered.

Margo could hear the sirens as they gradually filled the entire air with impatient buzz. She knew things would become difficult to explain afterwards, but she really didn't care anymore. She was with her husband now and he really didn't care about what he saw in the envelope.

Margo closed her eyes and allowed the darkness to consume her.

52809914R00064